Sharp as Lemons

Poetry

Mooring		1
Tributary		2
After the Storm		3
House for Sale – Quiet Location	Jacqui Rochford	4
The Problem		5
The Fallen		6
Time is a Delicacy	Andrea Tang	7
Living for Art, Living for Love	Roger Elkin	8
Nerves of a Leaf		10
A Messenger Empties his Sack	Mandy Pannett	11
Your Money or your Life		12
Scrap	Caroline Stockford	13
Lydia Dwight, dead	Marilyn Francis	14
Fractured		15
Pilgrim Souls in the Garden, after Dark		16
Tipping Point		17
Chris Hadfield's Photos of Earth from Space	Jan Harris	18
Still to Shed	Emma Teichmann	19
The Old Man Upstairs	Michael Law	20
Bringing Down the Wall	Phil McNulty	21
Mr Wheeler Belly	Anthony Kenehan	22
Invidious	Heather Buswell	23
Huzur Vadisi		24
Capetown 2002		25
Singing and Writing at the Lake with Roger		26
Back Packing to Symi – Resistance off Greece	Heather Williams	27
Chilling Night		28
Digging for Victory	Caroline Oakley	29

Arabian Eagle		30
Inheritance	Keith Shaw	31
Unravelling	L F Roth	32
Onion Ring	Laura Guthrie	33

Flash Fiction

Stag Night	Jeanne Davies	37
Summertime	R J Allison	37
Creep	Sue Clark	38
Pointless Platypus	Sasha Brown	38
Pruning the Past	Phil McNulty	39
Re-Education	Frances Colville	39
The Catch	Jeff Jones	40
The Man in the Sea	Antony N Britt	40
Decision		41
Thursday Evening	John Holland	41
What Remains	Emily Price	42
An Apple and a Tennis Racket	Sue Clark	42
Car Parks		43
Crow	Bronwen Griffiths	43
Rooster and Rat		44
The Glass House	Andrea Tang	44
For Sale	Dave Drummond	45
Changing Room	Jill Clough	45
Best Day of My Life		46
Kyushu, Japan	Trish Leake	46
Fairytale Ending	Meredith Jones	47
Care in the Community	Jaqueline P Vincent	47
Ant	Laura Guthrie	48
Contemplation	Maree Teychenné	48
The Human Body is More than 50% Water	Ian Shine	49
Deep, Calm Breath	Mark Nightstone	49
Careers Guidance	Laura Guthrie	50

Sharp as Lemons

Prizewinning Poetry & Flash Fiction

Earlyworks Press

Copyright Information

This anthology and cover design copyright © 2013 Kay Green. Copyrights to all works remain with their individual creators. All rights reserved. No part of this publication may be reproduced, stored in a retrieval system, rebound or transmitted in any form or for any purpose without the prior written permission of the author and publisher. This book is sold subject to the condition that it shall not be lent, resold, hired out or otherwise circulated without the publisher's prior consent in any form or binding other than that in which it is published.

Chris Hadfield's Photos of the Earth from Space by Jan Harris was first published on Poetry 24 blog, 21 May 2013

Trouble Man by John Holland appears in the Marble City Publishing anthology **Knife Edge**. Published in May 2013, all profits go to The Book Trust.

ISBN 978 1 906451-95-0

Printed in Hastings, UK
by Berforts Ltd

Published by Earlyworks Press
Creative Media Centre, 45 Robertson St, Hastings,
Sussex TN34 1HL

Email: services@earlyworkspress.co.uk

www.earlyworkspress.co.uk

Part One

Poems

Time is a Delicacy

You sprinkled seconds
over melting minutes,
licking your fingers, cat-like.
The steaming scent of
hour-stuffed days drew you,
dog-sniffing, mouth watering.
Mashed months rolled
into balls of years,
seasoned with
winter flakes,
spring blossoms,
summer rays
and autumn leaves,
had you swine-ing,
christmased you with Santa's pounds.
Then your appetite
slugged down,
caterpillared into a hole.
You looked in the fridge,
saw only scraps of calendars,
foul-smelling, going bad, left.
You sit down for your last supper,
before you,
a whole clock served on a silver platter,
its hands slow
to a standstill,
suddenly,
you're no longer hungry.
Around you,
the crumbs of yesterday
remain.

Andrea Tang

Living for Art, Living for Love
Auntie Reenie sings *Vissi d'arte* from *Tosca*

Classic Nite and at the Club's upright piano
sits Bob Pierce, tall and swarthy with more than
a touch of the negro in him, that's why he can do
that gravely Satchmo take-off folk regularly demand …

but tonight he's accompanying Reenie's spot –
her standing, hands clasped, operatic,
crimsoned lips pursed and primped, hair perm-rinsed,
waved, curled, crimped, and eyes glinting …
her stance that half-angled shoulder pose
she's seen at the *Theatre Royal*, head erect,
breath kept ready, then once Bob has insinuated
the intro, goes glowingly into song…

> *I lived for art, I lived for love*

Her voice
pouring sweetly, ringing like fine wine
and laddering the staves, a sort of
honeyed spun thread treading the scales

> *I sent up my song to the stars, to the skies*

not a warbling, but pure and fulsome,
though despite her heaving chest, her mouth's
bright flowering, not quite making it, the top notes
sliding and cracking

> *Why oh Lord,*
> *Why do you reward me thus*

And your mum's shoulders lifting
in cringing embarrassment (though staying
dumb) while sister Flo hisses *Christ!*

And, as the applause water-falls, Reenie's
breathing freely again, nodding Bob acknowledgement
till flashes a glance at husband Les that sends him
scarpering off, glass of Bass in hand,
to fetch her her second Cherry B,
all the while the barstaff humming

Why do you reward me thus

Roger Elkin

Nerves of a Leaf

I am un-leaving
in the pushing wind

and you
my feckless, temporal stem

would let me
detach, un-
loose my green dependence.

Now I will be rich
with autumn
tooth and saw-like
in my gloss

for this day

is muscular, not
a brown-crackle moment for shedding:
see how an early sun
shines.

Mandy Pannett

Lydia Dwight, dead

I saw you one Sunday afternoon
behind the glass in the museum
laid out on your stoneware deathbed,
a posy clasped in your cherub hands,
your face wholesome as a currant bun.

You were six. No one knows why you died,
children didn't always last in those days. Lydia
plain-faced Lydia, resting forever on salt-glaze
lace, final as a full stop.

Who would have thought to see you displayed
to Sunday gawpers. You are so small and homely
I think your father must have cast you for himself,
and I wondered what he might have made
of the Ancient Greek (with curly hair)
sharing space with you.

Marilyn Francis

Fractured

It's a delicate performance, she finds,
to balance on a swivel chair
and test the ceiling-mounted smoke alarm.

One push of the button and she plummets
to the ground, among cake crumbs,
dog hairs, flakes of eggshell paint.

She shakes like baking parchment
in a fan-oven till paramedics
gather her onto their trolley.

In A and E they slit her clothes with scissors,
spray her shocking-pink with antiseptic,
poke plastic pipes into viens.

Surgeons mend her bones with titanium
and send her home to clank from room
to room, a dayglo villain from Marvel

who sifts through particles of dust,
floor sweepings, fragments of bone,
for the person she used to be.

Jan Harris

Pilgrim souls in the garden, after dark

In this borrowed light we are half-way from life,
unable to see the colour of evening primrose,
the scarab's oily shine as it scuttles away.
Here, shapes are indistinct and pipistrelles
flit through open doors I can't perceive.
Your features blur, erased as night deepens.

Yet there are signposts in this place,
beetles look to the stars to find their way,
wax moths are lured by fragrances unfurled
when sunlight is softened by reflection.
As we linger on the seat beneath the oak,
I hear your thoughts and hope you hear mine.

A book lies between us, its poetry lost to darkness
though the beauty of Yeats' words still sings.

Jan Harris

Tipping point

We grieved when the Holm oak fell
in another record-breaking storm,

not for the bough which cradled our child's imagination
as she powered towards the chequered flag,
superbike hero on her Yamaha,

or the gable end reduced to rubble,
our wardrobe doors open to the sky
clothes snagged on twigs,
like prayer flags in the wind.

We sorrowed for the loss of certainty,
for benevolence turned to destruction,
for something unstoppable which howled in the gale
and tore the very roots of our existence.

Jan Harris

Chris Hadfield's photos of Earth from Space

Sunrise is a sequin poised
on the bolt of silk that wraps the Earth
in blue. Islands are luminous snails

or exclamations marks
shouting 'Look'. The Outback,
an abstract from the walls of The Tate.

Lights reveal where people live,
cobweb cities with roads that snake
or divide neighbourhoods into blocks.

Patterns emerge. Deserts, ridged and whorled
like human skin under a microscope.
Perspective shifts. Near and far are one.

The camera fails to catch
the grinding heat of sand, the tug
and pull of wind through hair

but shows the desolation of the Aral sea,
grit in the eyes of storms, our place
in a universe too vast to understand.

Looking up, we see the astronaut
behind the lens. The scientist, teacher,
poet, most of all, the man

who searched within himself
to find the courage for his voyage
and then reached out to carry us along.

Jan Harris

Still to Shed

I slithered out the womb a rotten brute,
Was coached in vicious ways by schools of snakes
Who bit with lie-stained teeth, whose hands would take
The fruits of unkind labour, who'd recruit
Poor peers who daren't refuse the tempting taunts
And who, in truth, would hanker for a part
In dessicating souls; their cankered hearts
They'd shutter, while their plundered bones they'd flaunt.
And I was one, was popular, was they
And them and those who understood the joke
Of youth – we'd incite fights, not thoughts provoke;
Swing dumbly, blindly, beating, through the day.
I had become a free and frothing God
Of death and dread, a snorting over-dog.

The smart of shame, the soreness of regret
Now presses on the larva of my soul,
So newly formed; and I cannot console
Myself – and I, with many years ahead,
Don't know a cure, an analgesic that
Will stop this pain which trounces through my breast;
Repentance seems mere selfishness redressed:
I plead forgiveness so my former brat
Can rest in peace and I can feel I've done
Enough. No! Rather I be shunned and cast
Away, and should the pain decide to last
Then it's deserved, despite what I've become.
For, truth be told, I finally am transformed:
Not yet a butterfly, but yet half-formed.

Emma Teichmann

The Old Man Upstairs

There he is again
stamping and raving
with his lewd laughter
up in the attic
tripping a bumpkin's dance
over the floor-boards
swilling the brandy-bottle
hurling his crutch
shouting obscenities
up to the cobweb rafters . . .

Down in the white
and gold drawing-room
someone is still
playing andante.
The family sits in the
pale decorous silence
of stiff-necked chairs
hands in their laps
waiting and waiting for
the pianoforte's tinkle
to destroy that
wicked old man upstairs
praying for God
to crush him
in his foulness
and leave the world
a cleaner tidier place
where everyone can
hear Haydn again.

Michael Law

Bringing Down the Wall

When the phone rang, I was stacking bricks.
Dry eyed, I listened to his tears.
A sense of shock, but no real surprise.

'I'm sorry to tell you this, he's dead.
They left a message on your answerphone,' he said.
'Oh… Thank you, for letting me know.
It was very good of you.'

Turning back, to the outhouse wall,
I swung the sledgehammer,
Through a brick cloud of sibling rivalry,
And, into the cracks, pushed a crowbar.
Levering masonry apart, fracturing
To tumble in untidy heaps
Amongst the dry, worthless, powder of lime mortar.
Then, in a dementia of shovelling,
I drove the damaged steel edge
Into our debris, into all that remained.
The madness and rubble of life too long lived.

I gripped the barrow handles tight
Pushed the load to the front of the house.
To the yellow skip.
And another load to the yellow skip.
And another.
I didn't know what to do then and I don't now.
Apart from keeping the barrow run clear and getting on with the job.

Phil McNulty

Mr Wheeler Belly

Wheeler Belly! Wheeler Belly!
Perhaps he's packed away the jelly.
And the ice cream. And 3 packs of Space Invaders.
Look at him in the school dinner queue.
Waiting for portion two.
Got detention twenty minutes with him, room B2.
But his dissemination of William the Conqueror's conquest of England really does merit his strong points as a teacher at this institution.

Anthony Kenehan

Invidious

The contempt is almost palpable
with a need to find expression
strong as the force of water
seeking outlet.

It lurks there, silent, invidious
demonstrated in small acts of
casual insurrection.
Calculated

methods of sticking up two fingers
yet remaining untouchable:
the insolent challenge
of wordless "so there."

There's little acts of vandalism:
gates are blatantly left open
the message: "nothing you can
do about it."

The fear is, one day, an eruption.
Man steps from Two Finger Building
with a gun, and there will be
a shooting here.

Heather Buswell

Huzur Vadisi

Sea breeze off the Azure coast greets
'the peaceful valley'.
Lying in a Turkish hammock
shoals of leaves on olive trees
turn and flash their underbellies
lifting light.

Swimming through the ages.

Compact and effervescent
holding shadows.

Turning them solid.
Reflecting sun confuses outline.

A hint of breeze
(gentle motion of the air)
sees the fish shimmer and dart.

Thoughts and memories
of nothing special.

Heather Williams

Capetown 2002

Atlantic breakers off a numbing sea,
blemish free hot dazzling sand.
An afternoon of beating heat
has trapped me in a torpid mood
until across my neutral gaze
his lean and shining
body
thrills   elementally
in movement.

Ebony cartwheels thru the shallows.
Uplifting pink soled feet.
Runs fast up
down
then up again
He plunges in
calmed instantly.

Climbs,
still wet, into his workmens blue.
Picks up his bike and wheels it off.
Playful and subordinate in one move.

He leaves me musing on apartheid.

Heather Williams

Writing at the Lake with Roger

Passing over passing away.
Warm wind blown clouds rolled up the valley
and across the resting land.
Voice hits rock, rebounds on air,
resonates in space above the lake.

Consider the sheep
As they eat and sleep,
then eat again
whilst we in vain
seek who we are –
exploring noble expression.

Persistent gusts of wind
and rounded melody drift overhead.
Soundless dragonflies unlikely motion.
Soundless clouds the shape of life,
all absorbed into the water.

Timeless the home of bleached bone.

Heather Williams

Back Packing to Symi – Resistance off Greece

Wrapped tightly in a blanket of heat,
we leave the port to climb up cobbled streets
where times go forward as time goes back.
Past houses cruelly blinded, doors and windows
filled with stones. We pant and plod our way to god,
heading for a smug white church that sits above.

The universal black clad sweeper
protects the gate of her domain. Keeps
stone as clean as history.
So the eternal day begins to shimmer, catching
momentary breeze that stirs the pines
to banish it from where it came and leave
the solemn job of keeping clean, of steps and lamps.
We pulse the path back down.
Upon us now the world will stop.
The sea sucks in its breath.

Our war is lost. My comrades stand on either side.
Symi is inside of me. Her walls behind
hold heat and fear and pain and grief.
We do not want to leave
the shining sky, the lovely life.
My hat, my hands.

A look   last look.

The shots

We drop   hard stone.

This memory I give to you to take back home
and weep.

Heather Williams

Raindrops falling like tiny battering rams
on his head. Hat no protection
against these cold, hard,
peppermints from heaven.
Reminders from the Ice Queen
of things that remain to be done.
Slowly he bends beneath the onslaught.
Picking up glittering shards and fallen leaves
to decorate the evening, make it
somehow special.
It's been a long day of nothing done
but wondering.
Where is he? Will he be there
when I get back?
Before the ice melts, the leaves dry
to a crisp, easily crushed
in anxious fingers.

Caroline Oakley

Digging for Victory

Lumpy, glutinous mud sticking to my boots,
buttons gritty and cold, slippery
beneath the stubs of my fingernails.
You know why I'm out here
toiling away, cutting sods,
turning over the soil.
It's where I come to get stuck in
to the problems you bring.

Counting the raindrops, the plinking
from the guttering, nature's water torture.
Drip, drip, drip on the brim of my hat.
Matching the drip, drip, drip of your scorn,
the poke, poke, poke of your laughter.

I think hard about the size of the hole,
the scheme and the planting. The depth
and the width. Longer than deep?
No more thumping. Only flowers.

Caroline Oakley

Arabian Eagle

Once a harmless ball of fluff:
a vulnerable chick, now Teflon tough
with wicked eye, body loaded
        from talon to beak with bombastic rhetoric.

High above the dry dust of the desert,
        soaring into a clear blue sky,
the male, clever and sly, will act as a decoy:
executing a series of mesmerising acrobatics
while its partner homes in on
        a seemingly bedazzled, unsuspecting, prey.

As they prepare for takeoff,
their razor-sharp beaks and claws glint
in the scorching afternoon sun,
        all hope of a negotiated settlement – gone.

Keith Shaw

Inheritance

    The wind had sheathed its spears of ill fortune,
        the summer garden breathing a brief contentment.
    Evening sunshine had thrown a garland
            of vermilion over a small circle
of soft lawn, when two collar doves,
        heads erect, delicate in their silky costumes,
were walking round each other,
            almost on tiptoe: ballet dancers,
performing a stately minuet of courtship,
        hearts fluttering, feathers slightly ruffled.

Death came suddenly: a whistle of wind,
        the last rays of sunlight reflecting
the black sheen of bullet-proof wings: magpies
        swooping down from dark cypress trees,
their beaks as vile and merciless
            as malice: a shaking and tearing,
a screech of pain – oblivion.
        Within minutes all that remained on the grass
were discarded scraps of claw and bone,
        a few feathers in the arms of a fitful breeze.
God said the meek shall inherit the earth:
            we are still waiting.

Keith Shaw

A drop, a dab
of something
used to stop the thread
as it began
to come undone.
Now she wears none.
Does anyone?
Do they even exist?
A list.
She should have made a list
of all that's gone.
How else hold on?
And if not gone,
then wobbly, shaky, from
that broken rung.
Her mind for one,
where concepts
have become
so hard to find.
Words hide, collide
and trick her tongue.
Stocking, she says. Nylons.
But what comes out
is not even a near rhyme:
aeons. An open sea of time.
She floats, for now.
One day, she knows,
the weave will be so worn
that she will drown,
each tear taking her
further, ever further, down.

L F Roth

Onion Ring

Onion ring.

Onion text,
onion email,
onion even write by snail mail

but garlic never reply.

Onion gonna cry.

Laura L J Guthrie

Part Two

Flash Fiction

Stag Night

She was frocked in innocence with long stilettoed legs.
   The predators watched her turn her graceful neck, head tilted to listen to the song. The light caught her vanilla hair and her purity drew us in. Sad globes adorned with long lashes flickered, unaware that we watched. Every man there wished he could strip her naked and keep her to himself.
   Suddenly she sprang into an evocative dance, shifting from side to side. The turmoil of her moves amplified the intense craving of her audience.
   I didn't pursue her but called my dog, un-cocked my gun, and walked home.

Jeanne Davies

Summer Time

It was one of those timeless summer days when the past feels present; one of those moments of irrational conviction that this day, this summer evening, doesn't just seem like one from the half-remembered endless summers of childhood, but actually is one – a perception that all such special, magical evenings are in fact the same evening. A vision of the thing flickered at the corner of my mind's eye; a theory, almost, scratched softly at my understanding. I turned the last bend in the familiar path, stepping out of the woods, and it was so.

R J Allison

Creep

'You sure it don't creep you out?' I go.

Molly shakes her head. 'You're like Harry Potter and his lightning bolt scar. Different.'

'Is that why the girls stare and scream?' I say, faking a laugh. 'They think I'm Daniel Radcliffe.'

'Is it a birthmark?'

'Hemangioma. Had it since I was little.'

She leans in, tracing her finger down the mark. The world goes still. I feel normal.

'Anyway,' she goes, 'a concealer would probably cover that.'

A dog yaps, a passing boombox motor thumps out hip-hop.

So much for not being creeped out. So much for being normal.

Sue Clark

Pointless Platypus

If a platypus walked in, it's unlikely that anyone would be surprised. At least, no one would be more surprised, after hearing the conversation prior to its entrance. Perhaps they would be more surprised, but already surprised thus, their resultant surprise would be higher than without the conversation, if the platypus simply walked in. Perhaps their destiny was to reach the aforementioned surprise, which would be fulfilled on the platypus' entrance without the conversation. It remains, however, that due to the conversation that happened (not the platypus that didn't) everyone in the room – lacking a platypus – was surprised.

Sasha Brown

Pruning the Past

The dogs are barking and it's there again, in our hedge.
　You can't say I'm dreaming. I see it moving, shaking, clipping, pruning.
　Slipping between privets.
　On Monday, I thought I saw a hand taking birdseed, filching peanuts.
　Yesterday it pulled in plastic bags. Made a shelter of dead leaves and woven branches, still sparse 'til summer's growth.
　I see a slender shape. A vaguely crouching form. I'm old enough for answers.
　What did happen to Mum all those years ago?

Phil McNulty

Re-Education

The gulls let her soar with them high above the sea, wheeling and diving, seizing the moment and drifting on a puff of air. They taught her to float, relaxed and oblivious on the rise and fall of the tide, to mew softly or to rend the air with raucous cries. Amidst the sweet aroma of rotting seaweed, they made her disdain those who offered titbits or tried to frighten her away. Then, having shown her the meaning of life, they left her to live her new freedom.

Sometimes they return to her roof to remind her.

Frances Colville

The Catch

He was skulking menacingly in a shop doorway, searching for a target. I should have turned and gone another way, but I was running late.

He was onto me in a flash.

From the moment we made eye contact my fate was sealed.

I tried to escape by walking quicker, but this was his turf.

Flustered, I took a wrong turn and ran into his mates. They never hunt alone. I was trapped.

I turned to confront my pursuer. He was grinning triumphantly knowing that I was cornered.

This was one market research survey I'd have to endure.

Jeff Jones

The Man in the Sea

'Shelley, do you see him?'

'Where?'

'There, by the water.'

'Yes. Who is he, Rufus?'

'That's Norman,' Rufus said, 'ready for his morning dip in the sea.'

Shelley licked salt from her lips, picked blonde strands which were stuck to her face. She watched Norman drop his towel, step in the water, wading until ankle height.

Norman lifted his head to the clouds, chanted. Sang to the island.

'He's 110 years old,' Rufus said. 'Not an ache in sight.'

Shelley's mouth dropped. 'Blimey. Time's stood still for him.'

Rufus laughed. 'Yes. Time waits for Norman.'

Antony N Britt

Decision

God came to them in the night. Moved amongst them. Made His decision known. When they met they agreed there was no choice. It was God's will. Despite their personal doubts. Their strong reservations. But the deals still had to be done. The negotiations completed. Promises made. Gifts distributed. Their own futures planned. Protection put in place. Eventually, they cast their votes. The ballots were burnt. Smoke billowed from the Sistine Chapel. The crowds stared.

God looked down. Quite right, He said. The bloody place is burning down.

John Holland

Thursday Evening

On Thursday evening, the caretaker, Mr Simpson, shy, fit, 50, armed with courage, went to the office of Mrs Beddows, 35, the school head. He told her that he cared for her.

Mrs Beddows reminded him that he was her employee, that she was married, and that their ages differed greatly.

Mr Simpson, the caretaker, emailed on Tuesday with the words "Forgive me, Mrs Beddows. I am trying to extinguish the fire in my heart."

Mrs Beddows replied, "Thank you, Mr Simpson." Below this, to cushion the message, she added above her name "Take care."

John Holland

What Remains

The mobile spun to the tune of the grandfather's finger. The solar system shuddered. Stars, moons and planets swung through the universe in desperation trying to fill the void that had been left behind. Beneath, the crib lay stargazing. Beside it, hills of new Babygros spread and dipped across the rug ready to be folded and put away. Bows and ribbons melted into soft cream carpet, forming puddles. The grandfather's finger tip rested against a dip in ceiling plaster before travelling to the mobile and pulling it gently down. There was no need for it any more.

Emily Price

An Apple and a Tennis Racket

The first time, all I took was an apple and a tennis racket. I didn't know any better. The apple to eat, the tennis racket for protection.

I met a man who said he was looking for his puppy but I didn't go with him. I tried to sleep but they moved me on with a broom, like a scrap of litter. So I ate the apple under a dripping bridge. Then I went back.

As I slipped into bed beside my brother, I heard it chime ten. No-one noticed I'd run away.

Sue Clark

For Sale

He picked them up, put them on his scattered desk and stared out the window. Carefully writing down the address he opened a bubble wrap envelope and placed them inside. It needn't have bothered him after this long – he'd put it off long enough. But it still stung. A man named Gerry was the recipient – baby's shoes, never worn. In all of his life, working his minuscule frame to breaking point in fields and factories, never did he imagine that his unborn child would have turned out to have such large feet.

Dave Drummond

Changing Room

'I'm ready for something different.'
    'What do you fancy?'
    'Something more streamlined. Younger-looking.'
    We survey the models. 'What do you think of this?' I point out a sleek outfit, black shot through with copper.
    'That'd be different. Shall I?'
    'What will Dan say?'
    'He'll certainly notice the difference.'

The assistant follows her into the changing room. I wait.

It's a change, definitely. My middle-aged, pallid friend is transformed into a leggy Afro-Caribbean beauty. I'm considering the Thai number beside me, glistening black hair, tiny hips, almond skin. Do they remodel the old bodies, I wonder? My turn next.

Jill Clough

Best Day of My Life

Imagine you're sitting in a rock pool of hot steaming water outdoors beside the sea. You're with three close friends passing around a bottle. Music is playing softly and every now and again, a wave washes over the rim of rocks into the pool. Oh and, did I mention the covering of snow on the rocks, the bright winter sunlight and the flawlessly clear blue sky?

Just close your eyes and imagine…which friends would you chose and what drink and music would you play?

And by the way, no clothes allowed in the pool.

Trish Leake

Kyushu, Japan

OMG, ten more steps. The god-awful smell makes my throat close.

Grey dust, grey cinders, and small grey pig-farm tin huts. Eyes tired of grey, I rest them in the pure cloudless blue sky. Crunching my way to the edge, I look down into an infinity of grey with flashing flickering red and I wobble. Signs tell me the tiny tins are in case of eruption.

Two busloads of tourists pull up and they swarm around me. I turn and count the tin huts…twenty. There's a rumble and the ground shakes.

I've never moved so fast.

Trish Leake

Fairytale ending

The repossession broke her heart, but her pension had lost half its value and she couldn't afford the big house any more. We moved her into the spare room of our semi, but she faded fast, pining for her home under the oaks where all you could hear were the birds and the brook. Even the kids couldn't cheer her up any more.
 Not long after she died, I walked past the old house and saw a sharp-suited man with hungry eyes climbing into a cab. "RBS," he said, and I thought, "That's who ate grandmother."

Meredith Jones

Care in the Community

Unopened bills clutter her kitchen table. Thud, driiinnnng. Kelly flees in dread to the bathroom, slams the door and bolts it.
 "Come on open up, we know you're in there." Kelly sits shaking, tears trickle and splash onto the cold tiled floor "we've got a warrant." A smashing of glass and splintering of wood announces the front door has burst its frame. Scuffing, grunts, heavy treads then silence wraps the small flat.
 "Kelly?" The voice soft echoing. "Those bastards! They've taken everything, come on honey, I've left a message for your social-worker."

Jaqueline P Vincent

Ant

There was an ant in my bed the night before last. Wouldn't normally bother me, but I'd made a jam sandwich for a late night snack and he kept pestering me for 'just one bite'. Also, he talked in his sleep. Something about holding the fort and marshalling the troops. And 'God Save the Queen'. Hardly got a wink. But worst of all, he was gone in the morning and never called me back.

Laura L J Guthrie

Contemplation

I often meditate while I do my hand-washing. It's the clarity and purity of warm soapy water, I think.

So yesterday, while I washed my large white bloomers (as nuns often do on a gloriously peaceful Sunday afternoon), I began to formulate plans for my newly-acquired, self-propelled narco submarine. Oh, what a gift the Lord has given me with the misplaced church funds! What joy a new hobby can bring and what hope can be extracted from this new-fangled trade of drug-running – beds, meals and warm clothes for the homeless!

Yes, the Lord does truly work in mysterious ways!

Maree Teychenné

Careers Guidance

"Why *ufology*? Why not something normal?"
"I'm fascinated by the unknown."

An honest answer would have involved recounting a long history of subtle snubs form classmates, increasing estrangement from family, strange looks from neighbours and neighbours of neighbours, and comments from teachers which, on the surface of it, were simply polite acknowledgements – but which also served to draw attention to 'odd' personal interests and pursuits, exhibiting them like acts in a freak-show. But even knowing that, the reason would have seemed naïve and stupid to him.

She held his gaze. "Sorry, can't help you there, and neither can anyone else. Time to move away from fantasy and consider a *real* career, I think."
"Ufology's a real career! There are whole files dedicated to individual cases. Someone must have to investigate them. It'll just take a bit more organisation, that's all. And if I have to create my own opportunities, I will."
"Well, I tried."

The door closed. The footsteps faded. The advisor stood up, locked the door and turned one of his shirt buttons through one hundred and eighty degrees.
"Pegasi, we have a problem…"

Laura L J Guthrie

~~ **The End** ~~

The human body is more than 50% water

There was a law passed that all tears must be shed into pots. Once filled, the pots were emptied into the town's communal drum, which had appeared shortly after the first accident. Once the drum was full, its contents were piped to a generator. This turned the lights back on, and people could start living again. They could watch TV, listen to music, party. Soon enough the tears dried up, and the power went with them. The street lights failed, emergency services stalled, and then came another accident.

Ian Shine

Deep, Calm Breath

Kirsty brushed back her hair, looked in the mirror and sighed. She dawdled before deciding to wear something a little formal with a flash of blood red. She adorned her mouth with her favourite pale lipstick. "It's going to be okay," Kirsty murmured. She took a deep breath and set her phone to vibrate before dropping it into the deep black, leather handbag. She slowly descended the stairs and pushed her feet into the shiny shoes with the small heel. "Deep, calm breath," she said. Her chest rose and fell. She forced a smile. Kirsty was ready.

Mark Nightstone

About Earlyworks Press

Books

Earlyworks Press lists include popular and contemporary poetry books, literary and genre fiction including science fiction and fantasy, and books about Hastings (the original home of the press). All our books can be ordered from independent bookshops, High Street and online, by post or direct from the website.

Club

The website is also the home of the Writers' and Reviewers' Club – a private, online forum where members can develop and polish their work and help each other to find markets for it. The club promotes members' fiction and non-fiction books and artwork on the website, on review sites such as **www.booksy.co.uk** and around the country at book fairs, readings and festivals.

Competitions

If you are a writer and would like to submit work for the next book, you can do so via our regular open competitions. There are also web-based competitions for fiction, micro fiction and poetry, and occasional genre challenges, usually offering bigger prizes and single-author publication contracts.

Go to the **Competitions Page** on the website for details. Sign up for the e-newsletter or visit **Earlyworks Press** on Facebook, follow **@CircaidyGregory** on Twitter or write, enclosing an SAE, to Kay Green, Earlyworks Press, The Creative Media Centre, 45 Robertson Street, Hastings, Sussex TN34 1HL

If you would like to join in our online workshops, use our services to writers or have space on our website to promote your own writing or artwork, please visit the Club and Stepping Stones pages at...

www.earlyworkspress.co.uk

Discounts and special terms are available, for the authors we publish and for competition winners, on all Earlyworks Press books and on club membership. Please email us for details.

Tina sang in her bedroom.
Tina sang in the kitchen.
Tina sang all over the house.
Her voice was DREADFUL, but her Mum
thought she was wonderful.

1

When she sang she had a voice like a shovel
clearing snow from a road.
But she still sang in her bedroom.
She still sang in the kitchen.
She still sang all over the house.
But her Mum thought she was WONDERFUL and
she bought her a guitar.

2

She sang in the bedroom with her guitar.
She sang in the kitchen with her guitar.
She sang all over the house with her guitar.
But it was even more dreadful than a shovel
clearing snow from a road.

3

She sang in the sitting-room and the budgie
dropped down dead.
She sang in the kitchen and all the glasses broke.
But her Mum thought she was WONDERFUL.
"What a voice!" she said.

Tina sang all over the house and played her guitar
and the neighbours shut their windows.
She sang in the garden and played her guitar, and
the neighbours moved away from their houses.
Her voice was so DREADFUL.
But her Mum thought she was WONDERFUL.
"What a voice!" she said.

Tina sang in the street.

Everyone shut their windows in the street.

Tina sang and sang and all the windows in
the street broke.

But her Mum thought she was WONDERFUL.

"What a voice!" she said.

Everyone in the street came out.
Tina sang for them all and played her guitar.
But it was even more dreadful than a shovel
clearing snow from a road.
All the people covered their ears.
And they moved away from their houses.

Tina went to a football match and she sang
to the crowd.
All the crowd covered their ears.
All the players covered their ears.
They could not play football.
Tina sang on and the ball BURST!

Tina sang at work. She was so happy.
All the workers covered their ears and they could not work.
So Tina was sacked.
But her Mum thought she was WONDERFUL.

Mum said Tina should go on a holiday to Switzerland.
She went and she was so happy on holiday.
She went up a mountain.
At the top of the mountain she yodelled in the snow.

But her yodel was like a shovel clearing snow from a road.
Rocks came off the mountain.
All the snow came off the tops of the mountains.
And all the people went away.

She went into a forest in Switzerland.
She was happy in the forest so she yodelled.
But her yodel was like a shovel clearing snow
from a road.
All the tops came off the trees of the forest.
And all the birds dropped down dead.

She went back home to her house and her Mum.
But there were no neighbours.
There were no people in the street.
So she sang because she was lonely.
Everyone in the town covered their ears.

13

But her Mum thought she was WONDERFUL.
She said, "Sing to me, Tina.
Yodel to me, Tina."
Tina sang and she yodelled.
"What a voice!" said Mum. "It is like the birds
in spring."

But all the people of the town came to Tina.
They said, "Please move away.
All our glasses are broken.
And all the windows of the town
are broken.
Please go away!"

So her Mum sent her to a lonely lighthouse out
at sea. When there was a fog at sea the
lighthouse men said, "Sing, Tina."
She sang and the singing cleared the fog. It all
went away.
And all the sailors were safe when the fog
was cleared.

The lighthouse men were happy as the fog
went away.
The sailors were happy as the fog went away.
The town was happy as Tina was away.
Everyone was happy.

17

But Tina was not happy.
She was lonely on the lighthouse out at sea.
She was so lonely . So she sang and she played
her guitar when there was no fog.
And all the sea-birds dropped down dead on
the lighthouse.

18

Her Mum was not happy as she missed having her in the house.
She missed having her singing.
She missed her guitar.
But everyone in the town said she could not go home.

So Tina joined the army.
She was happy in the army so she sang to all
the soldiers.
But all the soldiers covered their ears.
They said her voice was like a shovel clearing
snow from a road and she should go home.

Then a top man in the army had an idea.

He sent Tina to war.

She sang to all the soldiers in the war.

She sang and played her guitar to the soldiers.

21

All the soldiers in the war covered their ears.
They could not fight if Tina sang.
If Tina sang and played her guitar no-one
could fight.
And they all thought she was wonderful.
WONDERFUL!

TINA - YOU'RE WONDERFUL!

All the people in the town cheered Tina when
she got home.
Her Mum cheered and cheered as Tina was home.
"There will be no more wars," the people said.
"There will be no more dreadful wars."
They said, "Sing to us, play to us, Tina.
Rock on!"

23

Tina sang and played her guitar.
All the people in the town covered their ears.
But they all thought she was WONDERFUL.
They said, "Tina, you are TOP OF THE POPS."